Pun Choi

a hotchpotch of Chinese
folk and fairy tales

by Jane Houng

U0106752

QX PUBLISHING CO.

Pun Choi: a hotchpotch of Chinese folk and fairy tales

Author: Jane Houng

Editor: Betty Wong

Illustrator: Bianca Lesaca

Cover Designer: Lau Hing Cheong

Published by:

QX PUBLISHING CO.
8/F, Eastern Central Plaza, 3 Yiu Hing Road, Shau Kei Wan, Hong Kong

Distributed by:
SUP Publishing Logistics (H.K.) Limited
3/F, C & C Building, 36 Ting Lai Road, Tai Po, N. T., Hong Kong

Printed by:
Elegance Printing & Book Binding Co., Ltd.,
Block A, 4/F, Hoi Bun Industrial Building, Hong Kong

Edition:
First edition, December 2016
© 2016 QX PUBLISHING CO.

ISBN 978 962 255 117 6

Printed in Hong Kong.

This book is dedicated to Harriet and Rebecca,
both lovers of traditional tales from all over the world.

AUTHOR'S NOTE TO PARENTS

If you want your children to be intelligent, read them fairy tales. If you want them to be more intelligent, read them more fairy tales.

Albert Einstein

Fairy tales have universal appeal, as do folktales, fables, ghost stories and legends. They often highlight complex human conditions, often raise thorny moral dilemmas. Readers feel compelled to interpret, imagine, and predict. These skills are the root of inspiration, creativity and vision. I think that's why the most famous scientist who ever lived believed that fairy tales were so beneficial to children.

For this collection I have selected interesting stories from a wide range of traditional Chinese tales and retold them in modern settings for the enjoyment and edification of today's readers.

Jane Houng

October 2016

Contents

How:

What:

What if ...

Growing Wings

One sunny day the rice was sprouting, the birds were singing and a farmer's daughter sat minding ducks. *Splash!* An egret landed on the pond and the ducks rose to the sky, flapping and honking. *How I wish I had wings*, thought the girl. She stood up and raised her arms.

A teacher's daughter overheard her. 'Have wings? What a stupid idea,' she said. But when she arrived home, she dripped water on her shoulders and stood outside her block of flats.

'What *are* you doing?' asked her school friend, a businessman's daughter, who laughed cruelly when the teacher's daughter told her. 'If anyone had wings, it would be me. *My* family is rich.'

As soon as the rich girl arrived home, she rubbed massage oil on her shoulders and stood in her garden. The sunshine felt uncomfortably hot. 'Water! Bring me some water!' she called to her maid.

An official's daughter was watching from the balcony of her bedroom next door. '*My* family is both rich *and* powerful,' she said, 'so my wishes always come true.' Then she skipped back inside, sneaked into her mama's bedroom and sprayed her shoulders with the finest French perfume.

The Chinese dragon spotted her standing beside her family's swimming pool a few days later. He'd heard about the hundreds of Hong Kong girls turning brown as berries in the summer sun and had swum up from his watery

palace to see them with his own eyes. *If I give wings to all of these girls, there'll only be boys left. So I'll only give them to the first girl who wished for them,* he decided.

Did you see that? Someone flying as high as the hawks above the harbour? Someone swooping and somersaulting like a model aeroplane? It's the farmer's daughter.

The Boy who Played the Flute

There were once three orphaned brothers. When the eldest brother became a man he married a mean wife. The middle brother married a kind one. And the youngest brother, still a boy, married no one.

The eldest brother was responsible for taking care of his younger brothers. But he worked such long hours that the duty fell on his wife's shoulders. She took every opportunity to goad the youngest brother for being lazy. 'I've had enough of him,' she announced to her husband one day. 'It's time he was independent. Hire a *kaido* and dump him on the nearest island.'

In order to please his wife, the eldest brother did what she demanded. He ordered a boatman to sail him and his youngest brother to Shek Kwu Chau. Then, while his brother was exploring the beautiful island, he ordered the boatman to take only him back home. Without even a backward glance, he sailed away.

Meanwhile, the youngest brother had discovered friendly goats, cats and dogs. He gazed out to sea and laughed at the playful pink dolphins and diving birds. Then he walked back to the beach where the *kaido* had moored, and waited, and waited. The sky glowed pink and the sea turned grey before he realised he'd been abandoned.

But the boy was brave and he didn't mind being alone. He ate some fruit and slept curled up inside a cave. The following morning, he played his flute, which he always carried in his pocket. Sometimes he played it all day, with

the sunshine glistening on the sea. Goats, cats, cows, dogs, crabs and crayfish gathered to listen. Sometimes pink dolphins peeked from the sea to listen too.

So if you happen to be travelling to Macau one day, look carefully, because you may see them all.

The Wild Goose

There was once a fisherman who lived on the wetlands of Mai Po. While returning from fishing one day, he saw a plump goose with one wing spread awkwardly across the sand. It was injured.

The fisherman carried the goose home and nursed it back to health. On a beautiful summer morning, he released it back into the wild.

Soon after, he came home to find a pretty woman mending his nets. He invited her in and soon they were married.

At first his wife was happy, but gradually her cheeriness turned into seriousness, their conversations turned into silence. When the fisherman set off early one morning, he noticed a big black hawk circling his home. On his return, he found his wife crying.

The next morning, the hawk swooped down on him, cawing and pecking. The fisherman grabbed a brush and chased the bird away. His wife was watching and when he tried to comfort her, she cried more loudly. 'Forgive me for not telling you,' she said, 'but I'm not human. I once turned myself into a goose but got injured. That's when you found me. I came to be your wife to repay your kindness. But now we are in great danger because my father didn't agree with me. He has turned himself into a hawk in order to peck us to death.'

The following morning, the fisherman caught the hawk and tried to kill it. It flew away and stopped coming. His wife started to go outside to enjoy the sunshine again.

But one night the fisherman returned home to find it empty. With a heavy heart, he walked down to the beach. There, spread over the sand, was the crumpled body of a goose.

The poor old fisherman never smiled again.

The Haunted Flat

There was once a man who bought a flat at a very good price. The flat was second-hand but smelt new. Its wooden floor was beautifully polished. Its kitchen was sparkling white.

The man picked up the keys and stayed there the very first night. In the bedroom there was a double bed, a cupboard and a sofa. The sofa was pink and looked very soft. When the man sat on it to remove his socks, the fabric turned the colour of flesh and moved.

The man jumped up. Maybe he was imagining things because the sofa looked normal again. He unbuttoned his shirt and opened the cupboard to hang it inside. On one hanger hung a collection of colourful silk ties. The

man reached to touch a spotty blue one and it slithered into the shape of a slippery snake.

'Help!' cried the man.

The snake disappeared into a hole in the corner of the room. Without switching the lights off, the man ran out of the flat.

The next day he contacted a property agent. 'Yes, the flat is available for rent immediately. Yes, everything is in excellent condition,' he said.

Within a week, a tenant moved in. He was a construction worker who needed a good rest after a long day's work. He lay on the sofa and fell asleep almost immediately.

When he awoke, he saw two tiny half-naked coolies carrying a sedan chair. The man rubbed his tired eyes in disbelief as the midgets lowered the chair and delivered a tiny coffin. Its lid opened and a dainty lady dressed in white appeared. She held her sleeve to her face and sobbed.

The man tried to stand up but a cloud of fog surrounded him. The fog was cold and clammy and thick. 'Help!' he shouted.

No one ever saw him again.

Human Bait

Have you heard of Tiger Mountain near Tai O? The mountain got its name in the olden days when wild tigers still roamed around Hong Kong.

An old lady lived with her grandson in a nearby fishing village. One day she woke up with a fever. 'Climb up Tiger mountain and pick some *bajiao* for me,' she said.

The boy knew the way to the star anise trees because, when his grandmother could still walk, he'd often helped her pick medicinal plants. He walked up the mountain and filled his sack with nuts.

On his way down, there was a thunder-storm. The boy sheltered in a pagoda where he lay on a bench and fell asleep.

He awoke to find someone holding his hand: it was a hairy giant with a long beard and fat stomach. 'Let me go,' shouted the boy. But the giant pulled him into a cave.

A fire was burning. A lump of meat sizzled on a spit. The boy trembled. But the giant hooked the meat with a huge fork and sliced some meat for him.

The boy enjoyed a very tasty supper.

The next morning the giant strung some rope around the boy and carried him to a cliff. A tree trunk was wedged between two rocks. 'What are you doing?' cried the boy, afraid again.

Chuckling, the giant wrapped the boy around the trunk then hid behind a rock. The boy was hanging like human bait!

Scuffle, scuffle. What was that?

A tiger.

Bang! The giant clubbed the tiger, released the boy, and dragged the carcass back into the cave.

That night they had another feast.

'Can I go home tomorrow?' asked the boy, remembering his sick grandmother.

'Yes,' grunted the giant, 'As long as you promise to come back to help me hunt every Saturday night.'

An Eggy Tale

There was once a Chinese woman who had a great shock when she gave birth. That's because she didn't deliver a baby. She delivered an egg, with tiny arms and legs.

'Please don't eat me,' said Eggy. 'I'll be a good son, I promise.'

The wife and husband came to enjoy Eggy's good humour. Mr. Wong would carry Eggy in his pocket whenever he went out. He was buying vegetables at the street market one afternoon when a beautiful girl passed by.

'Papa, she's my soulmate,' said Eggy. 'Please arrange for me to marry her.'

Mr. Wong guffawed. How could that be possible?

'It is, and you will,' said Eggy.

So Mr. Wong arranged to meet the girl's father. Mr. Kong roared with laughter at Mr. Wong's request. 'On three conditions,' he said. 'That your egg buys my daughter a luxury house, a Porsche, and a diamond necklace.'

Eggy's parents thought the matter finished. But on hearing the news, Eggy brightened.

That night they spotted him digging up a flower bed.

Next morning their dining room table was laden with precious jewels. 'A businessman secretly buried them during the war,' explained Eggy. 'He's dead now, so these are all ours.

Let's go shopping!'

Mr. Kong choked on his snake soup when he heard what had happened. His beautiful daughter cried for three days. But the marriage went ahead.

On the wedding night, Eggy lay on the bed. A red light suddenly circled him and he turned into a handsome young man.

The newly-weds spent a lovely night together. But by dawn the boy had turned back into an egg.

'Crush his shell to keep him human,' said Mr. Kong, pleased to see his daughter happy again.

Which is what she did, the very next night.

But the moment the shell crumbled in her hand, the boy vanished and only an egg remained.

Through the Eyes

This may be the craziest story you will read today. It takes place on Lantau Island, where locals have farmed for centuries. Living off the land with a diet of fresh fruit and vegetables, the villagers are all healthy and strong.

There was once a husband and wife who grew food for their family. One year, one of their papaya trees grew so big that a patch of spinach below was in constant shadow. The wife called a boy to help her chop the tree down.

'I *could* help,' said the boy, 'but it will consume a lot of my energy. So please first feed me ten bowls of *congee* and a hundred dough sticks.'

The wife ran home to tell her husband, who, although surprised, quickly boiled a wok

of rice, and fried a stack of *you tiao*.

As the wife was pulling a cart laden with goodies towards the boy, a skinny girl approached. 'I'm very hungry,' she said. 'Could I have some?'

The wife took pity on the girl. But next minute the girl had gulped down the rice porridge, gobbled down the *you tiao* and was running away.

'Where's my food?' asked the boy, pointing to the empty cart.

The wife pointed to the fast-disappearing girl. The boy angrily ripped the papaya tree up, roots and all, and gave chase.

The girl ran and ran, ran to the next field where an old man was threshing rice. 'Farmer, hide me,' she cried.

'Jump into my right eye,' said the man.

Which the girl did.

But the boy jumped in after her.

So the girl ran across the bridge of the old man's nose into his left eye, landing close to a group of men played *mahjong*.

She jumped out.

As far as I know, the boy is still chasing her. I wonder if you have seen them.

The Journey of Two Worms

There were once two worms. The big
brother was a do-er. The little brother was
a thinker. One day, the big brother heard of an
old worm who could turn them into dragons.
'Let's go and find her!' he said.

The two worms set off across the rice
paddy. Sure enough, they bumped into the old
worm. 'I will turn you into dragons,' she hissed,
'but first you must obey me. Dig this mud!'

The worms set to work immediately. But
six months later they were still digging. It was

dirty, grimy, gritty work and the worms began to argue. 'We're no closer to being dragons than when we started,' complained the big brother. 'I think that old worm is a liar.'

'Hush,' said the little brother. 'It's rude to talk like that.'

'At least we could ask her how much longer we have to suffer.'

The little brother finally agreed.

'You are indeed near the end,' said the old worm. 'Tomorrow you can set off for the lake. Before you reach there, you will come to a large field which needs plowing. Plow for one hundred days then you can crawl down to the lake.'

But the plowing was even more tiring than the digging. On the ninety-ninth day, the big brother had had enough.

As he crawled down to the lake, a big rain cloud covered the evening sun. *Crash!* There was a clap of thunder and the worm wriggled faster. Then lightning flashed and he felt rain pounding his back, his face blowing up like a

moon. His head had turned into a dragon but what about his body? He was almost drowning in the downpour.

Quickly, he slid inside a cave.

The next sunny morning, in the distance, he saw his little brother transform into a magnificent dragon.

The big brother felt so embarrassed he hid inside the cave forever.

Herbal Healing

There was once a sister and brother whose mama was very sick. The poor children couldn't sleep for worry, until a Chinese doctor told them about some medicinal herbs that might help her get better. 'They grow on a mountainside near an old smuggler's cave on Cheung Chau,' he said.

When the children set out it was raining cats and dogs and the ferry ride was roller-coaster rocky. But the children found the cave. Herb bushes blossomed around its mouth.

They stuffed their rucksacks with sweet green stalks and turned to go, when – *snatch!* – something grabbed them from behind by the scruff of their necks and pulled them into the cave.

The eyes of a hairy monster and the flames of a fire glinted in the darkness. A half-eaten dog was turning on a spit and the air was thick with smoke. The monster sniffed the herbs and sliced them with his steel-sharp claws. 'You'll taste even juicier sprinkled with these,' he said.

'We must get home. Our mama is sick,' pleaded the boy.

But the monster only rubbed his lumpy belly and burped.

The girl stood on her tiptoes, making herself as tall as she could be. 'How dare you plan to eat us,' she said. 'It wasn't even you

who caught us.'

'Let me prove it,' roared the monster, startling the bats hanging above. Flapping what looked like a dirty bed sheet, he hid his ugly face behind it.

Oddly, both the monster's face *and* the sheet disappeared.

The girl laughed. 'Show us one more time!' she said.

The moment the monster hid again, the children tugged the sheet out of his grasp and ran away underneath it.

The herbal soup cured their mama's illness.

The Young Man who Couldn't Catch a Ghost

There was once a woman who lived in a New Territories village. Every night the most delicious smells would float from her kitchen window. Every weekend all her sons and daughters would visit her and she would roast a whole pig on a spit. Her neighbour, a young fisherman, became curious about how she had enough money to eat so well.

The woman explained: 'One night I was walking through the cemetery and I saw a ghost. I screamed and ran. But it seemed the ghost was more afraid of *me*, because when I looked again, it had turned into a pig. So I caught the pig, carried it down the mountain, and have caught lots of other pigs since.'

The young man couldn't believe his luck. For now he knew that ghosts could turn into

pigs which could be eaten. *I too could have free pork forever,* he thought.

That very night, he carried a sack, a club, and some rope into the country park. The crescent moon smiled at him from the night sky. He stood in front of a grave and waited for a ghost to appear.

He waited and waited, growing stiff with cold. Mosquitoes bit his arms. A snake slithered by. At dawn he gave up and went home.

After that, he went out ghost-hunting every night, for week after week. Once he saw a flash of light in the trees and ran after it, but it was only a shooting star.

After a couple of months, he gave up.

So it seems that ghosts only come out when people are frightened of them. The young man in this tale wasn't frightened so the ghosts were too scared to haunt him.

Making Humans

Here in the civilized world, strange things can happen before our very own eyes.

There was once a man who drew up his van near a village house on Lantau Island. It was a scorching day and there was no wind. 'I need a room for the night, dinner, and somewhere to tie my dogs,' he said to the owner of the house, an old Hakka woman.

She helped him tie his five huge dogs to her gate. They were panting heavily. 'Don't give them anything to drink,' said the man sternly, as he drove off to park his van.

The dogs pawed the ground. The woman felt sorry for them. Nearby there was a shady banyan tree. *I'll tether them there,* she thought. But on the way, the dogs spotted a river and dragged her down the bank to drink. The moment water touched their lips, they transformed into five girls.

'Who are you?' said the old woman, brushing mud off her lampshade hat.

But it seemed they couldn't talk. And then the man was coming back! The woman quickly hid the girls behind the tree.

Behind the man, being pulled by him, were five fat sheep. He immediately asked the old woman where his dogs were. 'I'll bring them to you after I've cooked your dinner,' she replied craftily.

She tied his sheep to her gate then walked towards her house. The man followed her. He ordered the finest steamed fish and a selection of vegetables for his dinner.

'I'll go and fetch your dogs now,' said the woman, when all his dishes were on the table.

The wise old woman had a suspicion. She quickly untied the sheep and led them to the water. The moment they drank, they transformed into five boys. That's when she knew the man must be an evil magician.

She phoned 999 and the police came to arrest him.

A Hong Kong Tiger Tale

Once upon a time, wild tigers roamed Hong Kong mountains. So when a boy fell into a tigers' pit, he thought he would die.

Three cubs were playing in the deep muddy hole. The boy squeezed into a crevice and said his prayers. The sky above darkened and an evening wind rustled the trees.

Then a strong smell filled the air: the cubs' mother had brought home her kill. A wild boar drooped from her bloody mouth. She jumped down into the pit and, ignoring the boy, ripped the animal up while the excited cubs waited their turn.

The cubs ate until they couldn't eat anymore. One juicy boar chop remained – one of the cubs pushed it to the boy with his nose.

The next night, the tiger mother came back with a barking deer. The cubs ate to their fill, leaving the boy some belly meat. He washed it down with some rainwater he'd collected in his boot.

A month went by and the cubs grew big. One morning they jumped onto their mother's back and she leaped up to ground level. The boy once more feared for his life. 'Please don't leave me here,' he said.

The tiger let the boy grip her paws to pull himself up. So grateful was he that he promised her a pig. 'I will ask my father to roast one for you next full moon,' he said, hurrying home.

The mountain pathway lit up like silver the night the tiger and her three cubs padded down to his village. A villager smelled them and raised the alarm. People grabbed sticks, metal bars and torches.

'Stop!' cried the boy, and the father told his son's story.

Amazed, the villagers lay down their weapons and helped carry the pig to the tiger family.

The tigers ate it with gusto then disappeared back up the mountain.

Why...

Why do Chickens have Combs?

Do you know why chickens have combs? Let me tell you.

There was once a chicken who'd been invited to a chicken party. She put on her favourite feathery dress and admired herself in the water of a well.

Oo-er! How ugly her bald head looked. She couldn't go looking like that!

That's when she remembered the beautiful red hat the eagle owned. Maybe her friend would let her borrow it.

The eagle was a kind old bird. 'Of course you can,' she squawked.

During the party all the other birds gathered around to compliment the chicken on how lovely she looked. How happy she felt!

Back home after the party, she had one last look at herself in the well water. How pretty she looked! Too bad she had to return that hat.

The next day she hid it in the woods, and waited.

Seven days passed until the eagle flew by. 'I'll have my hat back, please,' she squawked.

The chicken bowed her bald head. 'When I see you, I blush with shame,' she replied, 'because while I was coming back from the party, a strong wind blew your hat away.'

The eagle looked very disappointed.

The chicken squirmed inside. 'How about I give you my two legs as a replacement?' she said. 'After all, they were the ones who walked over to ask you the favour.'

'No, no,' replied the kind eagle, as the chicken knew she would. 'What good would that do?'

But a few weeks later, the eagle was flying

across the meadow when she spotted something red. She flew lower. The red dot became a spot. The chicken had her hat on!

The eagle's eyes glowed red.

She swooped down and gripped the hat with her beak. But the chicken flapped her wings and ran. The eagle swooped again, and missed. It seemed the hat was glued to the chicken's head! In frustration, the eagle tore it to shreds with her talons.

All that remained was a jagged mess and this is now called a chicken's comb.

Why do Goats go *Bleh*?

There was once a goat and a sheep who liked to drink together. They'd climb down a ladder from heaven to sip crystal clear water in fluffy white clouds.

One day, the weather was so fine the animals could see all the way down to Earth. 'Doesn't it look wonderful?' said the sheep, twitching her little tail. 'The grass is as green as the finest jade and the sea sparkles like sapphires. I bet the water is sweeter than honey down there.'

'It's an awfully long way,' bleated the goat, peering down the silver ladder.

Nightfall came. The sheep still wanted to go to Earth. She lowered her hoof to the first rung.

'I've heard that some humans can be cruel to animals,' bleated the goat.

'*I've* heard they're all very kind,' said the sheep. 'Why would they hurt *us*?'

The goat wasn't sure. But the sheep was his best friend so he followed her. Down, down, they went. The ladder led to a long golden chain which was great fun to twist and twirl in.

'*Bah!*' cried the sheep. 'I'm stuck!'

Some humans heard her cries. They untangled her, as well as the goat, and tied them to a pole.

'*Bleh!*' bleated the goat. 'I told you so.'

From that day on, the animals had lots of lovely things to eat and drink. Both soon grew fat. But the goat still wanted to go back.

'Why?' asked the sheep.

The next day they heard a new sound – a rasping, grating swish of knives being sharpened on stones. They smelled fire. '*Bleh!*' bleated the goat. 'See what they're doing? This is all because of you!'

The sheep didn't say a word. She felt so sad she hadn't listened to the goat.

And to this day, goats bleat a lot because they're always blaming sheep for luring them away from heaven.

The Arrogant Azalea

O nce a year, a flower queen invites flowers to her garden and awards a prize to her most beautiful guest. The azalea always attended.

'May I go with you?' asked an evening primrose.

The azalea rippled her gown of red petals. 'You're such a straggly little plant, all stalk and no flower. How dare you ask me to accompany you?'

'But my blossoms come out at night,' said

the evening primrose, flicking a tendril to wipe a dewy eye.

A hearty hibiscus bush overheard them. 'You can come with me,' he said.

'That's very kind,' replied the evening primrose.

'Good riddance,' said the azalea. 'And do go away. I need some beauty sleep before I leave.'

The flower party was in full bouquet when the hibiscus bush and the evening primrose arrived. Roses were dancing in the breeze. A row of strelizia were dancing the cancan. The evening primrose danced with them all and told them how pretty they looked.

The azalea arrived in full bloom but with a long face.

'You smell nice,' said a bee, buzzing above her. The arrogant azalea closed her petals so the bee couldn't drink.

The flower queen flew over to a banyan tree and all the flowers clustered around her. 'I award this year's most beautiful flower award ... to evening primrose!' she announced.

The azalea flushed crimson. 'She isn't even

in blossom,' she cried.

But the flower queen presented the winning flower with a beautiful crown of freshly-picked daisies. 'Evening primrose has the kind of inner beauty that never fades,' said the queen. 'She's such fun to be with and always finds the best in everyone.'

'But what about me?' said the azalea, shaking her petals.

No one paid her any attention, and as the sun sank behind the mountain the evening blossoms of the primrose shone like gold.

The Tiger Behind the Fox

In a country park all the wild animals were busily feeding before nightfall. The wild hogs were eating roots. The barking deer were drinking water. Monkeys were jumping from branch to branch grabbing fruit.

Crash! All the animals stopped for a moment. What was that? A tiger had caught a fox. 'Help!' cried the fox.

The tiger locked the fox in his jaws and loped down the path to his lair.

'How dare you think of eating me?' said the fox. 'I'm the king of the forest.'

The tiger lowered the fox to the ground, 'You?' he growled. 'I thought *I* was.'

'I'll prove it,' said the fox, 'if you let me take a walk with you.'

So they walked along the country path together, the fox leading the way.

First they met a barking deer. It raised its head, barked its distinctive bark, and ran back to the trees.

'You see? It's afraid,' said the fox.

They rounded a corner and bumped into a family of wild hogs. The hogs were the fox's friends and would usually grunt hello. Not this time. They quickly turned tail and bolted.

The clever fox led the tiger to his den. He'd burrowed it at the base of a boulder many moons ago. Palm trees masked the entrance. There they were filling their stomachs with freshly-plucked bananas.

Usually the monkeys chatted with the fox at dusk. This time they hooted wildly, jumped

away from tree to tree, disappearing into the park.

'You see? They're terrified of me,' said the fox.

The tiger was very impressed.

The fox pointed to the darkening sky. 'Oh look! What a beautiful moon tonight,' he said.

As the tiger raised his head, the fox raced into his den.

The Boastful Tortoise

There were once two egrets and a tortoise who were the best of friends. They lived by a lake and spent their days eating and swimming in the plentiful water.

But one year there was a terrible drought. The lake shrunk to the size of a dried plum. Fish died. Plants shrivelled. Whenever the egrets flew off elsewhere, the tortoise would ask them to bring some worms back.

A month passed and there was still no rain. Most of the animals and insects had already

left. 'We should leave too,' said the egrets. 'There's another lake nearby which we can fly to.'

The tortoise lowered his head. 'How can I move fast enough to keep up with you? I'm already weak with thirst.'

Then he had an idea. 'When you fly, could I hang on to the middle of a stick you're holding with your beaks?'

'Why not?' said one egret.

'Don't open your mouth on the way,' teased the other.

So the friends took off. They flew high over rolling mountains, swooped down to a village, swung past sacred temples. The tortoise felt full of wonder.

Down below, farmers were harvesting rice. One of them looked up. 'Those birds are carrying a tortoise. How clever of them,' he said.

The tortoise felt a bit hurt. After all, *he* was the one who'd had the idea.

Children laughed and pointed. 'How smart of the egrets. I wish they'd fly me like that.'

The tortoise gritted the stick angrily.

Then lots of villagers were milling, pointing, waving. 'What a great idea, birds!'

The tortoise couldn't bear the egrets getting all the praise anymore. He shouted, 'Hey, it wasn't—'

But of course, as soon as he opened his mouth, he fell like a rock from the sky.

'What a foolish tortoise,' the villagers said and continued on their way.

Miss Chongcao

If you ever travel to the mountains of Sichuan or Tibet, you may meet Miss Chongcao the caterpillar. She used to live on the plains. But there is a good reason why she now stays so high up.

Every spring, the fashionable Miss Chong-cao would crawl out of the earth and change into her favourite jade-green dress. Then she'd lie in the sprouting grass and enjoy the warm sunshine on her back.

One spring, she spotted a four-legged

creature. *Nibble, nibble!* It grazed from the edge of the plain towards where Miss Chongcao was hiding. 'Watch out, I'm here!' she called, tickling the horse's nose with her back end. 'If you eat me, you're sure to get stomach ache.'

The horse jumped backwards and trotted away.

That was lucky, thought Miss Chongcao. *Maybe I'd better look more like the insect I really am.* So she promptly changed into a brown velvet gown and spread herself out on a comfortable mushroom for an afternoon nap.

Scratch, scratch! What was that? Miss Chongcao opened her eyes and screamed. A golden pheasant was scratching the soft earth beneath her bed. It picked Miss Chongcao up, dangled her in its beak, tossed her in the air.

'Don't eat me!' cried Miss Chongcao. 'I'm

poisonous. Let me go!'

The golden pheasant was so surprised she dropped Miss Chongcao, who quickly wriggled away.

Nibble, nibble! *Scratch, scratch!* A few days later, Miss Chongcao heard the familiar

sounds of both the horse and the golden pheasant. Oh dear, what could she do? Squirm up the nearest mountain as fast as her tiny legs could carry her.

Living above the snow line, the fashionable Miss Chongcao still dresses in jade-green in spring and brown velvet gown in winter but is now safe from predators.

How ...

The Laziest Man in the World

Did you know that the laziest man in the world used to live in Hong Kong? He grew from a baby to a child to an adult, as we all do. The only difference was that he grew lazier and lazier the older he got.

When he was a baby, his mama fed and clothed him, like all good mamas do. But she was still feeding him every meal all the way through school, as well as dressing him. In the summer she would fan him while he played computer games. In the winter she would boil him chicken soup while he watched cartoons.

When the laziest man in the world became a man, he married. His wife cooked and cleaned and washed and ironed, like all good wives do. But she had to feed and clothe him too.

One day, his wife's mother fell sick. She lived in northern China a thousand miles away.

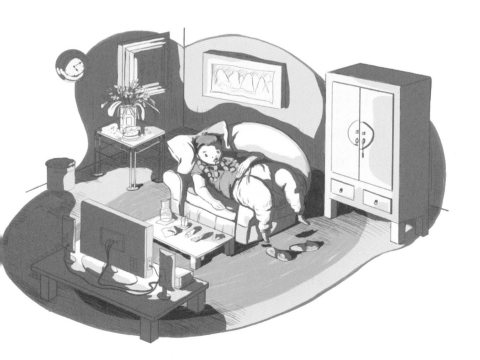

The wife worried about leaving her husband ... until she woke up in the middle of the night with a solution.

Next morning she baked twenty sweet rice cakes. With a sharp knife, she cut a hole in the middle of them and strung them on a string. Before she left for the train, she led her husband to the sofa and tied the necklace around his neck. 'Eat a cake a day for the next twenty and before you know it I'll be back,' she said. 'I won't telephone because I know you won't bother picking up.'

Her husband just blinked.

The man's wife nursed her mother back to health. But on returning home she found her lazy husband dead on the sofa. He'd eaten some of the cakes at the front, but none at the back.

He'd been too lazy to pull the string.

How the Misers Turned into Monkeys

There was once an old man and woman who were very rich but very stingy. Like many wealthy Hong Kong people, they had a domestic helper whom they worked to the bone. They ordered her to go to the market twice a day, as well as cook, wash, iron and clean. She even had to massage the old woman's feet for two hours after dinner.

The helper worked very hard and always tried her best to please but the old couple were never satisfied. They only gave her scraps to eat. Dinner, for example, was the rice stuck to the rice cooker she had to scrub clean every night.

Fortunately, the gods noticed how badly the helper was being treated and sent someone down from heaven to intervene. The girl was

scraping a wok one night when someone tapped at the kitchen window. It was a beggar. 'Please give me something to eat or I will die,' he said.

The kind-hearted helper gave him the rice she'd managed to scoop from the rice cooker.

'Thank you,' said the beggar. 'To reward you, here's a cloth. Wash your face with it twice a day.'

Which is what the helper did.

Day by day, the cloth worked its magic: the helper grew prettier and prettier.

It goes without saying that the old woman was very jealous. One day she couldn't resist asking some questions. When the girl revealed her secret, the woman seized the cloth, saying 'It's mine now.'

The helper protested but to no avail.

That afternoon the couple used the cloth to wash their faces.

'What's happening?' cried the old woman, looking in the mirror.

'Oh no!' said the old man, rubbing his arms.

Their bodies were sprouting long black hairs. They looked just like...well, you know, monkeys!

That night they caught the first plane to the jungle.

The Brown-nosed Eel

One summer morning, the sun shone brightly and a brown-nosed eel wriggled out from under a rock to swim in the sea. So happy was she that she didn't notice a snake. Open-mouthed, it swam towards her. Just before it clamped its jaws on its breakfast, the eel looked up.

'Stop!' she cried.

'Why should I?' hissed the snake.

'Look at my long twisting tail. It's like yours, because ... we're relatives.'

'Are we?' The snake retracted its poisonous fangs and swam away.

Laughing at her easy escape, the eel played in the cool water. But from the murkiness below swam an enormous shark. Its spiked teeth looked like daggers. '*A-ha*, a tasty fish,' it said.

Terrified, the eel tried to swim away. She dropped into the seaweed that blanketed the ocean floor, but became entangled. The more she tried to escape, the more entangled she became. 'Mercy!' she cried.

'Why?' said the shark.

'Sister shark, can't you see my fin trapped in the weed? You have a fin, and I do too. That's because we have the same ancestors. Won't you please save me?'

Being a polite shark, and believing the eel's lie, the shark tugged at the grass to free the eel.

'Thank you, dear sister,' said the eel, swimming away as fast as she could.

Feeling tired, the eel found a soft mound of golden sand and curled up for a nap. She awoke to swirling waters and a rushing sound. Opening her puffy eyes, she saw, coming straight for her, a giant swell with the snake and the shark both in it, both ready to tear her to pieces.

Quickly, the eel wormed her way underneath the sand. Which is why, unless you are very lucky, it is rare to see brown-nosed eels.

How the Deer Lost her Tail

Long ago on Lantau Island there lived an old couple. They were happy, gentle, contented people. Every morning the old woman watered the flowers in her garden. Every afternoon the old man fed his goldfish.

'Our life would be perfect if I weren't so scared of Tiggy,' said the old woman one night.

Her husband nodded.

Just outside, crouching against their front door, was a huge wild tiger. *Tiggy?* he thought. *Who's that?* Surely *he* was the scariest in the forest. Not someone called Tiggy!

Crash! Someone fell from the old couple's roof into their garden bushes. It was a thief who had lost his footing.

The tiger was terrified. He ran back along the path that led to the woods, accidentally knocking over a barking deer. 'Did you see that? It was Tiggy!' he said, as the deer scrambled to its feet.

'Tiggy? Isn't that y--?'

'*Shhhh,*' said the tiger, looking over to the garden.

The deer had never seen Tiggy looking so afraid.

As they tried to catch sight of whatever was climbing out of the bushes, the tiger caught a whiff of the deer's delicious body. 'Let's tie our tails together,' he said. 'We'll look more scary that way.'

The deer agreed, feeling much safer with a tiger beside her.

Crash! 'Ow!' someone cried. Another thief had fallen off the couple's roof.

'Tiggy!' roared the tiger and bounded off towards the trees.

Ouch! The little deer's tail snapped right off. But she picked herself up and ran into the woods too.

The front door opened. It was the old woman. 'No dear, I can't see anything,' she said to her husband. 'Those funny noises must have been the wind.'

The Fox Turns a Somersault

There was once a man who lived alone in a stone hut. Since losing all his money on gambling tables, he lived a quiet life growing vegetables. He dearly wanted a wife but couldn't afford one.

Little did he know but a kindly fox spirit had been watching over him for many years. One day, when the man was out, she climbed into his hut and changed herself into a woman. Then she raced around cleaning the floors, washing the man's clothes and cooking him a meal.

Click. At the turn of the front door key, she disappeared.

This went on for a while, until the man couldn't resist hiding under his bed to see who was coming through his window. Before long, he spotted the pointed nose of a fox. *Swish!* The fox did a somersault and landed on her feet in the form of a beautiful woman.

A fox skin lay on the floor. As soon as the woman went into the kitchen, the man seized the fur and hid it behind a wall.

The woman searched all over for her skin without success. So she sat down, and said, 'Now you know my secret, let me be your wife.'

The couple lived happily together for many moons. Then one day, while they were playing with their son, the man pointed to his wife and said, 'Do you know your mother is really a fox?'

The little boy clung to his mother and cried.

'Prove it!' said his wife angrily.

The man prised a stone from the wall to retrieve the fur, thinking that showing it to his son would make him laugh.

But as soon as his wife saw it she somersaulted, flipped back into the fox skin and raced through the door.

Nobody saw her ever again.

The Tiger and the Toad

O nce, a long time ago, a tiger was snuffling for food along a river bank. Birds clucked cries of danger. But one animal – a toad – didn't hear them because he was underwater. Poking his head out for air, he came face to face with the tiger.

'Good morning,' said the tiger, twitching his whiskers.

'How do you do?' said the toad politely, leaping on top of a large mound of mud.

The tiger wrinkled his nostrils. 'I'm fine. A

little hungry though. I haven't eaten for three days. Before I gobble you up, please tell me who you are.'

The toad blew up his belly as round as a ball. 'Call me the king of the toads. Because I can leap very far and do all kinds of amazing tricks.'

'You?' chuckled the tiger.

'Well, I bet I can jump farther across this river than you, for example,' said the toad.

'No chance,' said the tiger, crouching down to prepare.

The moment before the tiger jumped, the toad hopped on to the tiger's tail and bit into it.

The moment after the tiger landed, he looked back to the other side of the river.

'Here I am, silly!' croaked the toad, sitting on a boulder ahead.

The tiger snarled and pawed the air.

'Wait!' croaked the toad. 'I mean ... I bet I can spit more than you too.'

Not to be outwitted, the tiger accepted the challenge. But he hadn't drunk for a few hours so his spit was less than normal.

The toad spat out more – including a lump of hair from biting the tiger's tail.

The tiger growled in surprise. 'Why do you have so many tiger hairs in your stomach?'

The toad glanced in the direction of his spit. 'Oh those,' he said airily. 'They're from the animal I killed yesterday.'

'Good day,' said the tiger, and fled.

The Old Woman and the Monkeys

There was once an old woman who lived in an old shack near Shing Mun. She grew bananas, which the local monkeys loved. While she napped, they would jump over her fence and eat them. Their hooting usually woke her up.

But one hot day the old *tai tai* slept so soundly, she didn't hear them. When she finally awoke, she waved a rattan brush and shouted, '*Shoo!*'

But only three bananas remained on her palm tree. The old woman hobbled over and picked them. 'I'm ruined!' she cried. 'I've a banana for breakfast, one for lunch, one for dinner, then tomorrow I starve.'

Her house was near a market and her wails alerted a shopkeeper. '*Lao tai tai,* why do you cry so?' he asked. When he heard her story, he gave her some mats. 'Place them on your stairs tonight,' he said.

'Why should I do that?' cried the woman, as the man went on his way.

Her cries alerted a tailor. When the young lady heard the woman's plight, she gave her some pins. 'Scatter them around your mosquito net tonight,' she said.

'But why?' wailed the old woman.

Her wails alerted a spice man. He gave the old woman some chillies, saying, 'Rub your bananas with these, then sleep with the fruit under your pillow.'

The old woman thought the three people were quite mad but before she slept, she did exactly what they had told her to do.

That night, as expected, the monkeys sneaked through her window.

Ow! One monkey slipped and fell on the stair mats.

Aagh! The pins pricked a monkey's paws.

Only one monkey managed to reach the bananas. He could smell them under the old woman's pillow. He grabbed one and bit into it. *Yuk!* He spat it out, his mouth on fire with chillies.

The monkeys never bothered the old woman again.

What...

The Clever Judge

One cold winter's day, a poor farmer was carrying a bucket of rotten eggs, mouldy cabbage and smelly fish bones along a street. It was food for his pigs. In front of a tailor's shop, he tripped, and the contents spilt all over the pavement.

The tailor came storming out.

'Sorry,' said the farmer.

'*Pooh!* Clear up that mess,' shouted the tailor.

'I'll go and fetch a mop.'

The tailor wasn't satisfied. 'It smells so bad I demand you clear it up right away. Use your coat.'

'Please, no,' said the farmer. 'It's the only one I own.'

'Too bad!' shouted the tailor.

At that moment a judge was driving by. He

ordered his chauffeur to stop and stepped out of his car. 'What a stink! Why don't you clear it up, farmer?' he asked.

The farmer explained. 'Without my coat, I'll freeze to death.'

'Never mind. Use it,' commanded the judge.

Muttering unhappily, the farmer obeyed.

The tailor laughed unkindly.

'Happy now?' the judge asked.

'Yes!' said the tailor.

'So *your* case is closed,' said the judge. 'But the farmer's case is now open.'

'What?!' The tailor's eyes nearly popped out of his head.

'Look at him,' said the judge. 'He's shivering with cold. That cold could develop into pneumonia, which could kill him. If that happens, you could be accused of murder.'

'Oh, no,' said the tailor. 'What can I do?'

'Settle it out of court,' said the judge, 'by giving him a new coat right away. Go back inside your shop and pick the warmest coat you can find.'

The warmest coat was the most expensive. The farmer was delighted with it. 'Thank you,' he said, before going on his way.

The judge smiled at the tailor. 'Didn't I handle that case well?'

'Yes,' mumbled the tailor.

'You can't be too careful with troublemakers,' said the judge.

The Loyal Dog

There was once an old woman who lived on Lamma Island. Like many boat people who were carried on their mother's backs as a child, she had very bandy legs. But still, every month, her landlord demanded she travel into the city to pay her rent in person.

On the first day of May, a particularly hot day, the old woman packed a water bottle in her bag and set off to the ferry pier. 'Go home!' she ordered her dog, her only friend. They had lived together through typhoons and tidal waves and she loved him dearly.

The dog kept walking by her side.

The old woman sat on a rock by the road and pulled out her water bottle. Sweat dripped down her wrinkled face. She let her dog lap from her hand then ordered him home.

But at the ferry pier, the dog reappeared, wagging his tail and barking.

'Whatever is the matter with you?' said the old woman, waving her walking stick. 'You know you can't come into the city with me. Now, scram!'

She poked the dog's back, pushed him in the direction of home, but he still wagged his tail and yelped.

Toot, toot! The ferry was ready to depart. The dog scratched its paws on the concrete pavement and howled.

'I'll be back before dinner,' called his mistress.

The ferry bumped across the sea. The old woman felt sleepy. Before closing her eyes, she put on her glasses to count her cash one last time.

Eiya! Where was her purse? She checked her bag, her pocket, again and again, but couldn't find it anywhere.

When the ferry reached Central, she caught the next one straight back. On the way home, she hobbled past the place where she'd stopped to drink.

And there was her dog, sitting on a boulder.

He was guarding her purse.

The Flea and the Louse

F leas and lice used to live as one happy family. That's until one particular flea tried to trick one lousy louse. The two of them lived together in a crowded flat with lots of humans and pets to feed off.

One day, a grandmother came to live there too. She was so old and sick, she couldn't get out of bed. When the flea and the louse smelled her, they felt very happy. But the flea was a greedy pest who didn't want to share even a hair follicle with the louse. So when he saw his friend crawling up the old lady's neck, he planned a competition he was sure he could win.

'Here are the rules,' he said. 'Before the sun goes down, we'll make a pile of human hair.

The highest hair pile will win the old lady.'

The louse couldn't think of a better plan, so she agreed.

The flea flew off. With his long legs, he jumped around the flat collecting all the family's stray hairs. He was so confident he would win, he even sucked a little blood from a puppy while she was sleeping.

Meanwhile the louse, unable to jump or fly, slowly crawled around the old lady's bed, collecting what she could.

The sun slipped behind Sunset Peak. 'Time's up!' called the flea. He rolled the many hairs he'd collected into a ball and balanced it on his back. But when he jumped, it fell off.

The same thing happened many times. Then, when he finally managed it, while jumping back into the old lady's bedroom, he passed her electric fan. *Whoosh!* His precious hairs scattered far and wide and he wasn't even left with one.

'*Ha ha*, Grandmother's all mine,' said the lousy louse, sitting on top of her little mound.

Yum, yum. Grandmother tasted delicious.

The Grey Eagle

There were once two brothers who lived together. The elder brother was a mean man who wanted the house all to himself. 'Build one of your own,' he said to his little brother, 'and here's a bag of seeds.'

The younger brother meekly built a house, and planted the seeds. He watered them every day, but only one sprouted. His unkind brother had roasted all the others.

One morning, the man espied a grey eagle pecking at the only green stalk. 'Please don't,' he called.

But the big bird seemed desperate. 'I have three babies to feed,' she said, 'and there's no other food for miles.'

The man felt sorry for her, so let her eat.

'I will reward your kindness,' hooted the eagle as she spread her wings to fly. 'Be ready at dawn, with a sack.'

Sure enough, the next morning, the grey eagle appeared. 'Fly on my back,' she said.

She flew him to a magical mountain. Gold nuggets and precious jewels sparkled among the crops. 'Hurry,' cawed the eagle. 'We must leave before sunrise or we'll be burned alive.'

The man hurriedly gathered a sack of seeds. Once home, he planted them and they grew into a thick fields of wheat, corn and barley.

The elder brother couldn't believe his eyes when he came by, especially after he heard

what had happened. He went home, roasted all but one of a handful of seeds, and planted them. Then, when the grey eagle flew by, he allowed her to eat the only stalk and said he'd be waiting the following morning.

The second they reached the mountain, the man grabbed all the gold he could, adding rubies, sapphires and diamonds to his sack.

'Hurry,' said the eagle.

But the man ignored her.

So when the sun rose, the eagle flew away leaving the man to roast and burn.

The King of All Roosters

Before the threat of bird flu, Hong Kong people could raise chickens and the Chan family had a garden near Mui Wo where they kept some. Every morning, before school, Chan Junior rooted around the bushes looking for warm eggs. He had names for all the chickens and knew all the secret places where they laid. Feather, for example, laid behind a honeysuckle bush. Pecker in an old bucket. Fantail in an old Tanka hat.

But then there was Rob the rooster. He

didn't lay eggs of course. Instead, every morning, at the first streak of dawn, he would strut around the garden crowing *cockadoo-dledo*!

Now Rob had the longest tail feathers you could ever imagine and the most dashing red crown in town. And *chirp,* did he know it! Not

only would he crow *cockadoodledo, cockadoo-dledo* hundreds of times a day, but also other sounds which only chickens can understand. Like:

I'm your master
I'm your king
And you're my slave.

The chickens thought him a cocky fellow who was too big for his feet. So they kept well away from him.

But Mr. and Mrs. Chan were often driven mad by Rob's noisy morning calls. Mr. Chan would block his ears with cotton wool. Mrs. Chan would hide her head under the bed covers. Chan Junior, who was up anyway to collect eggs, would chase Rob around the garden with a rattan brush.

But even then, Rob's morning calls could be heard all around the village.

Cockadoodledo, cockadoodledo!

I'm your master

I'm your king

And you're my slave.

One morning, Rob crowed one time too many. Mr. Chan stomped out of the house, grabbed Rob behind the chicken coop and tied his beak shut with a bright red ribbon.

That morning Mr. and Mrs. Chan slept in peace.

Sources

Growing Wings
This is a Hong Kong retelling of a Chinese fairy tale called *Growing Wings,* published in the *Children's World Magazine,* issue 18, book 3, in 1926.

The Boy Who Played the Flute
This is a Hong Kong retelling of a Chinese fairy tale called *The Boy Who Played Flute* published in the collection *Min Qian Qu Shi* by the writer Bei Xin Shu Ju in 1933.

The Wild Goose
This is a Hong Kong retelling of a Manchu folktale.

The Haunted Flat

This is a Hong Kong retelling of the ghost story *The Haunted House* from *Strange Tales from a Chinese Studio* by Pu Song-ling.

Human Bait

This is a Hong Kong retelling of a folktale called *Yi Ren Wei Ni* by the writer Yuan Mei.

An Eggy Tale

This is a retelling of a Chinese folktale called *The Egg* published in the collection *Min Qian Tong Hua* by the writer Bei Xin Shu Ju in 1932.

Through the Eyes

This is a Hong Kong retelling of a Chinese folktale called *Through the Eyes* published in the collection *Min Qian Gu Shi* by the writer Bei Xin Shu Ju in 1933.

The Journey of Two Worms

This is a retelling of an ancient Manchu fable.

Herbal Healing

This is a Hong Kong retelling of a Chinese folktale which

was published in the collection *Ming Qing Tong Hua* by the writer Bei Xin Shu Ju in 1933.

The Young Man who couldn't Catch a Ghost
This is a Hong Kong retelling of the ghost story *Gui Bi San Mang* which was collected in *Fantastic Tales* by the writer Ji Yun.

Making Humans
This is a Hong Kong retelling of the ghost story *Making Animals* from *Strange Tales from a Chinese Studio* by Pu Song-ling.

A Hong Kong Tiger Tale
This is a Hong Kong retelling of the folktale *Yi Hu Ji* from a Qing dynasty collection called *Jiu Xiao Shuo*.

Why do Chickens have Combs?
This is based on an ancient Naxi tribe legend.

Why do Goats go *Bleh*?
This is based on an ancient Naxi tribe legend.

The Arrogant Azalea
This is loosely based on an ancient Naxi tribe legend.

The Tiger Behind the Fox
This is a retelling of the famous fable called *Hu Jia Hu Wei* from the book *Zhan Guo Ce*.

The Boastful Tortoise
This is based on an ancient Naxi tribe legend.

Miss Chongcao
This is loosely based on an ancient Naxi tribe legend.

The Laziest Man in the World
This is a retelling of a Chinese folktale, published in the collection *Ming Qing Tong Hua* by the writer Bei Xin Shu Ju in 1933.

The Misers Who Turned into Monkeys?
This is a retelling of a Chinese folktale, published in the collection *Ming Qing Tong Hua* by the writer Bei Xin Shu Ju in 1933.

The Brown-nosed Eel
This is based on an ancient Naxi tribe legend.

How the Deer lost her Tail
This is a Hong Kong retelling of an ancient fable originally from Southeast China.

The Fox turns a Somersault
This is the retelling of a ghost story from South China.

The Tiger and the Toad
This is the retelling of an ancient folktale originally from Southwest China.

The Old Woman and the Monkeys
This is a Hong Kong retelling of a Chinese folktale, published in the collection *Ming Qing Tong Hua* by the writer Bei Xin Shu Ju in 1933.

The Clever Judge
The idea for this story was borrowed from a legend about the writer Luo Guanzhong who wrote the famous historical novel *The Three Kingdoms*.

The Loyal Dog
This is a Hong Kong retelling of the legend *Yi Quan* from *Strange Tales from a Chinese Studio* by Pu Song-ling.

The Flea and the Louse
This is a retelling of a Chinese folktale, published in the collection *Ming Qing Tong Hua* by the writer Bei Xin Shu Ju in 1933.

The Grey Eagle
This is a retelling of an old Xibo fable.

The King of all Roosters
This is a Hong Kong retelling of a northern Chinese fable.